At Christmas play and make good cheer,
For Christmas comes but once a year.

KINGFISHER
An imprint of Larousse plc
Elsley House, 24-30 Great Titchfield Street
London W1P 7AD

First published by Kingfisher 1996
2 4 6 8 10 9 7 5 3 1
Copyright in this selection © Larousse plc 1996
Illustrations copyright © Sophie Allsopp 1996

A CIP record for this book
is available from the British Library

ISBN 1 85697 498 7

Printed in Hong Kong

THE LITTLE BOOK OF

CHRISTMAS

Selected by Caroline Walsh • *Illustrated by Sophie Allsopp*

Kingfisher

Contents

A CHRISTMAS-TREE SONG

The Chestnut's a fine tree
    In sunshine of May,
With blossoms like candles
    In shining array;
But they're not half so pretty
    Or so welcome to me
As the little wax candles,
Red-and-white candles,
Lighted four-a-penny candles
    On a little Christmas tree.
All trees in their season
    Bear fruits that are good,
In hedgerow or garden,
    In orchard or wood;
But they cannot show anything
    So delightful to see
As the brown-paper parcels,
Plump paper parcels,
Jolly ribbon-tied parcels
    On a little Christmas Tree.

RODNEY BENNETT

LITTLE TREE

little tree
little silent Christmas tree
you are so little
you are more like a flower

who found you in the green forest
and were you very sorry to come away?
see   i will comfort you
because you smell so sweetly

E.E. CUMMINGS

8

WAITING

Waiting, waiting, waiting
   For the party to begin;
Waiting, waiting, waiting
   For the laughter and the din;
Waiting, waiting, waiting
   With hair just so
And clothes trim and tidy
   From top-knot to toe.
The floor is all shiny,
   The lights are ablaze;
There are sweetmeats in plenty
   And cakes beyond praise.
Oh the games and dancing,
   The tricks and the toys,
The music and the madness
   The colour and noise!
Waiting, waiting, waiting
   For the first knock on the door –
Was ever such waiting,
   Such waiting before?

JAMES REEVES

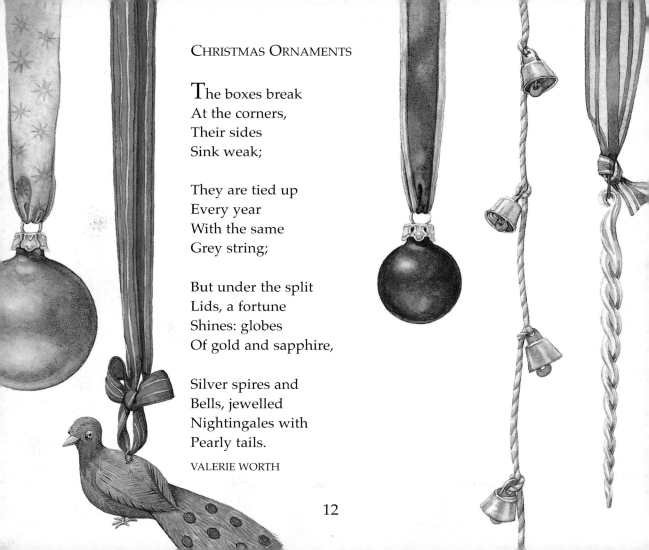

CHRISTMAS ORNAMENTS

The boxes break
At the corners,
Their sides
Sink weak;

They are tied up
Every year
With the same
Grey string;

But under the split
Lids, a fortune
Shines: globes
Of gold and sapphire,

Silver spires and
Bells, jewelled
Nightingales with
Pearly tails.

VALERIE WORTH

CHRISTMAS SECRETS

Secrets long and secrets wide,
brightly wrapped and tightly tied,

Secrets fat and secrets thin,
boxed and sealed and hidden in,

Some that rattle, some that squeak,
some that caution "Do Not Peek". . .

Hurry, Christmas, get here first,
get here fast . . . before we burst.

AILEEN FISHER

THE CHILDREN'S CAROL

Here we come again, again, and here we come again!
Christmas is a single pearl swinging on a chain,
Christmas is a single flower in a barren wood,
Christmas is a single sail on the salty flood,
Christmas is a single star in the empty sky,
Christmas is a single song sung for charity.
Here we come again, again, to sing to you again,
Give a single penny that we may not sing in vain.

ELEANOR FARJEON

15

CHRISTMAS AT MOLE END

(*from* The Wind in the Willows)

KENNETH GRAHAME

Sounds were heard from the forecourt without – sounds like the scuffling of small feet in the gravel and a confused murmur of tiny voices, while broken sentences reached them – "Now, all in a line – hold the lantern up a bit, Tommy – clear your throats first – no coughing after I say one, two, three. – Where's young Bill? – Here, come on, do, we're all a-waiting –"

"What's up?" inquired the Rat, pausing in his labours.

"I think it must be the field-mice," replied the Mole with a touch of pride in his manner. "They go round carol-singing regularly at this time of year. They're quite an institution in these parts. And they never pass me over – they come to Mole End last of all; and I used to give them hot drinks, and supper sometimes, when I could afford it. It will be like old times to hear them again."

"Let's have a look!" cried the Rat, jumping up and running to the door.

It was a pretty sight, and a seasonable one, that met their eyes when they flung the door open. In the forecourt, lit by the dim rays of a horn lantern, some eight or ten little field-mice stood in a semi-circle, red worsted comforters round their throats, their forepaws thrust deep into their pockets, their feet jigging for warmth. With bright beady eyes they glanced shyly at each other, sniggering a little, sniffing and applying coat-sleeves a good deal. As the door opened, one of the elder ones that carried the lantern was just saying, "Now then, one, two, three!" and forthwith their shrill little voices uprose on the air, singing one of the old-time carols that their forefathers composed in fields that were fallow and held by frost, or when snow-bound in chimney corners, and handed down to be sung in the miry street to lamp-lit windows at Yule-time.

> Villagers all, this frosty tide,
> Let your doors swing open wide,
> Though wind may follow, and snow beside,
> Yet draw us in by your fire to bide;
> Joy shall be yours in the morning!
>
> Here we stand in the cold and sleet,
> Blowing fingers and stamping feet,
> Come from far away you to greet –
> You by the fire and we in the street –
> Bidding you joy in the morning!

HIGH IN THE HEAVEN

High in the Heaven
A gold star burns
Lighting our way
As the great world turns.

Silver the frost
It shines on the stem.
As we now journey
to Bethlehem.

White is the ice
At our feet as we tread,
Pointing a path
To the manger-bed.

CHARLES CAUSLEY

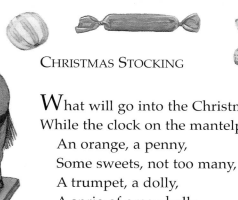

CHRISTMAS STOCKING

What will go into the Christmas Stocking
While the clock on the mantelpiece goes tick-tocking?
  An orange, a penny,
  Some sweets, not too many,
  A trumpet, a dolly,
  A sprig of green holly,
  A book and a top,
  And a grocery shop,
  Some beads in a box,
  An ass and an ox,
  And a lamb, plain and good,
  All whittled in wood,
  A white sugar dove,
  A handful of love,
  Another of fun,
  And it's very near done –
  A big silver star
  On top – there you are!
Come morning you'll wake to the clock's tick-tocking,
And that's what you'll find in the Christmas Stocking.

ELEANOR FARJEON

from A CHRISTMAS PACKAGE

My stocking's where
He'll see it – there!
One-half a pair.

The tree is sprayed,
My prayers are prayed,
My wants are weighed.

I've made a list
Of what he missed
Last year. I've kissed

My father, mother,
Sister, brother;
I've done those other

Things I should
And would and could.
So far, so good.

DAVID McCORD

I saw three ships come sailing in,
Come sailing in, come sailing in,
I saw three ships come sailing in
On Christmas Day in the morning.

And who should be in those three ships,
In those three ships, in those three ships,
And who should be in those three ships,
But Joseph and his Lady.

And he did whistle and she did sing
And she did sing, and she did sing,
And he did whistle and she did sing,
On Christmas Day in the morning.

MISTLETOE

Sitting under the mistletoe
(Pale-green, fairy mistletoe),
One last candle burning low,
All the sleepy dancers gone,
Just one candle burning on,
Shadows lurking everywhere:
Someone came, and kissed me there.

Tired I was; my head would go
Nodding under the mistletoe
(Pale-green, fairy mistletoe),
No footsteps came, no voice, but only,
Just as I sat there, sleepy, lonely,
Stooped in the still and shadowy air
Lips unseen – and kissed me there.

WALTER DE LA MARE

Under the Mistletoe

I did not know she'd take it so,
  Or else I'd never dared;
Although the bliss was worth the blow,
I did not know she'd take it so.
She stood beneath the mistletoe
So long I thought she cared;
I did not know she'd take it so,
Or else I'd never dared.

COUNTEE CULLEN

WINTER MORNING

Winter is the king of showmen,
Turning tree stumps into snow men
And houses into birthday cakes
And spreading sugar over the lakes.
Smooth and clean and frost white
The world looks good enough to bite.
That's the season to be young,
Catching snowflakes on your tongue.

Snow is snowy when it's snowing
I'm sorry it's slushy when it's going.

OGDEN NASH

COUNTRY CAROL

Walked on the crusted grass in the frosty air.
Blackbird saw me, gave me a gold-rimmed stare.

Walked in the winter woods where the snow lay deep.
Hedgehog heard me, smiled at me in his sleep.

Walked by the frozen pond where the ice shone pale.
Wind sang softly, moon dipped its silver sail.

Walked on the midnight hills till the star-filled dawn.
No one told me, I knew a king was born.

SUE COWLING

In the Bleak Midwinter

In the bleak midwinter
    Frosty wind made moan,
Earth stood hard as iron,
    Water like a stone;
Snow had fallen, snow on snow,
    Snow on snow,
In the bleak midwinter
    Long ago.

What can I give him
    Poor as I am?
If I were a shepherd
    I would bring a lamb,
If I were a Wise Man
    I would do my part –
Yet what can I give him,
    Give him my heart.

CHRISTINA ROSSETTI

CHRISTMAS IN THE SUN

Our Christmas Day is blue and gold,
And warm our Christmas Night.
Blue for the colour of Mary's cloak
Soft in the candle-light,
Gold for the glow of the Christmas Star
That shone serene and bright.

Warm for the love of the little babe
Safe in the oxen stall.
We know our Christmas by these signs
And yet around my wall
On Christmas cards the holly gleams
And snowflakes coldly fall,
And robins I have never seen
Pipe out a Christmas call.

MARGARET MAHY

DECK THE HALLS

Deck the halls with boughs of holly,
'Tis the season to be jolly,
Fill the mead cup, drain the barrel,
Troll the ancient Christmas carol.

See the flowing bowl before us,
Strike the harp and join the chorus,
Follow me in merry measure
While I sing of beauty's treasure,

Fast away the old year passes,
Hail the new, ye lads and lasses,
Laughing, quaffing all together,
Heedless of the wind or weather.

MINCEMEAT

Sing a song of mincemeat,
Currants, raisins, spice,
Apples, sugar, nutmeg,
Everything that's nice,
Stir it with a ladle,
Wish a lovely wish,
Drop it in the middle
Of your well-filled dish,
Stir again for good luck,
Pack it all away
Tied in little jars and pots
Until
   Christmas
      Day.

ELIZABETH GOULD

CHRISTMAS PIE

Lo! now is come our joyfull'st feast!
    Let every man be jolly;
Each room with ivy leaves is dressed,
    And every post with holly.
Now all our neighbours' chimneys smoke,
    And Christmas blocks are burning;
Their ovens they with bakemeats choke,
    And all their spits are turning.
Without the door let sorrow lie,
    And if for cold it hap to die,
We'll bury it in a Christmas pie.

ROAST GOOSE AT THE CRATCHITS

(from *A Christmas Carol*) CHARLES DICKENS

There never was such a goose. Bob said he didn't believe there ever was such a goose cooked. Its tenderness and flavour, size and cheapness, were themes of universal admiration. Eked out by the apple-sauce and mashed potatoes, it was a sufficient dinner for the whole family; indeed, as Mrs Cratchit said with great delight (surveying one small atom of a bone upon the dish), they hadn't ate it all at last! Yet every one had had enough, and the youngest Cratchits in particular, were steeped in sage and onion to the eyebrows! But now, the plates being changed by Miss Belinda, Mrs Cratchit left the room alone – too nervous to bear witnesses – to take the pudding up, and bring it in.

Suppose it should not be done enough! Suppose it should break in turning out! Suppose somebody should have got over the wall of the back-yard, and stolen it, while they were merry with the goose: a supposition at which the two young Cratchits became livid! All sorts of horrors were supposed.

Hallo! A great deal of steam! The pudding was out of the copper. A smell like washing-day! That was the cloth. A smell like an eating-house, and a pastry cook's next door to each other, with a laundress's next door to that! That was the pudding. In half a minute Mrs Cratchit entered: flushed, but smiling proudly with the pudding, like a speckled cannon-ball, so hard and firm, blazing in half of half-a-quartern of ignited brandy, and bedight with Christmas holly on top.

Oh, a wonderful pudding! Bob Cratchit said, and calmly too, that he regarded it as the greatest success achieved by Mrs Cratchit since their marriage. Mrs Cratchit said that now the weight was off her mind, she would confess she had had her doubts about the quantity of flour. Everybody had something to say about it, but nobody said or thought it was at all a small pudding for a large family. It would have been flat heresy to do so. Any Cratchit would have blushed to hint at such a thing.

At last the dinner was all done, the cloth was cleared, the hearth swept, and the fire made up. The compound in the jug being tasted and considered perfect, apples and oranges were put upon the table, and a shovel-full of chestnuts on the fire.

The holly and the ivy,
When they are both full grown,
Of all the trees that are in the wood,
The holly bears the crown.

The rising of the sun
And the running of the deer,
The playing of the merry organ,
Sweet singing in the choir.

The holly bears a blossom,
As white as the lily flower,
And Mary bore sweet Jesus Christ,
To be our sweet Saviour.

The holly bears a berry,
As red as any blood,
And Mary bore sweet Jesus Christ
To do poor sinners good.

The holly bears a prickle,
As sharp as any thorn,
And Mary bore sweet Jesus Christ
On Christmas Day in the morn.

The holly bears a bark,
As bitter as any gall,
And Mary bore sweet Jesus Christ
For to redeem us all.

SPIDER

I sing no song. I spin instead
High in the loft above your head,
I weave my stillnesses of thread.

I loop my wiring silver-clear,
to light your manger chandelier.
Listen! my web is what you hear.

NORMA FARBER

CHRISTMAS SPIDER

My fine web sparkles:
Indoor star in the roof's night
Over the baby.

MICHAEL HARRISON

Away in a Manger

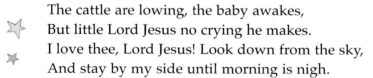

Away in a Manger, no crib for a bed,
The little Lord Jesus laid down his sweet head;
The stars in the bright sky looked down where he lay,
The little Lord Jesus asleep on the hay.

The cattle are lowing, the baby awakes,
But little Lord Jesus no crying he makes.
I love thee, Lord Jesus! Look down from the sky,
And stay by my side until morning is nigh.

CHRISTMAS MORN

Shall I tell you what will come
to Bethlehem on Christmas morn,
who will kneel them gently down
before the Lord new-born?

One small fish from the river,
with scales of red, red gold,
one wild bee from the heather,
one grey lamb from the fold,
one ox from the high pasture,
one black bull from the herd,

one goatling from the far hills,
one white, white bird.

And many children – God give them grace,
bringing tall candles to light Mary's face.

RUTH SAWYER

A CONVERSATION ABOUT CHRISTMAS

DYLAN THOMAS

Self: There were the Useful Presents: engulfing mufflers of the old coach days, and mittens made for giant sloths; zebra scarves of a substance like silky gum that could be tug-o-warred down to the galoshes; blinding tam-o-shanters like patchwork tea-cosies, and bunny scutted busbies and balaclavas for victims of headshrinking tribes; from aunts who always wore wool-next-to-the-skin, there were moustached and rasping vests that made you wonder why the aunties had any skin left at all; and once I had a little crocheted nose-bag from an aunt now, alas, no longer whinnying with us. And pictureless books in which small boys, though warned, with quotations, not to, would skate on Farmer Garge's pond, and did, and drowned; and books that told me everything about the wasp, except why.

Small Boy: Get on to the Useless Presents.

Self: On Christmas Eve I hung at the foot of my bed Bessie Bunter's black stocking, and always, I said, I would stay awake all the moonlit, snowlit night to hear the roof-alighting reindeer and see the hollied boot descend through soot. But soon the sand of the snow drifted into my eyes, and, though I stared towards the fireplace and around the flickering room where the black sack-like stocking hung, I was asleep before the chimney trembled and the room was red and white with Christmas. But in the morning, though no snow melted on the bedroom floor, the stocking bulged and brimmed: press it, it squeaked like a mouse-in-a-box; it smelt of tangerine; a furry arm lolled over, like the arm of a kangaroo out of its mother's belly; squeeze it again – squelch again. Look out of the frost-scribbled window; on the great loneliness of the small hill, a blackbird was silent in the snow.

Small Boy: Were there any sweets?

Self: Of course there were sweets. It was the marshmallows that squelched. Hardboileds, toffee, fudge and allsorts, crunches, humbugs, glaciers and marzipan and butterwelsh for the

Welsh. And troops of bright tin soldiers who, if they would not fight, could always run. And Snakes-and Families and Happy Ladders. And Easy Hobbi-Games for Little Engineers, complete with Instructions. Oh, easy for Leonardo! And a whistle to make the dogs bark to wake up the old man next door to make him beat on the wall with his stick to shake our picture off the wall. And a packet of cigarettes: you put one in your mouth and you stood at the corner of the street and you waited for hours, in vain, for an old lady to scold you for smoking a cigarette and then, with a smirk, you ate it. And, last of all, in the toe of the stocking, sixpence like a silver corn.

DING DONG! MERRILY ON HIGH

Ding dong! merrily on high
   In heav'n the bells are ringing:
Ding dong! verily the sky
   Is riv'n with angels singing.

Gloria, Hosanna in excelsis!
Gloria, Hosanna in excelsis!

E'en so here below, below,
   Let steeple bells be swungen,
And io, io, io,
   By priest and people sungen.

Pray you, dutifully prime
   Your matin chime, ye ringers;
May you beautifully rime
   Your evetime song, ye singers.

from THE NEW NUTCRACKER SUITE

A little girl marched around her Christmas tree,
And many a marvellous toy had she.
There were cornucopias of sugar plums,
And a mouse with a crown that sucked its thumbs,
And a fascinating Russian folderol,
Which was a doll inside a doll inside a doll inside a doll,
And a posy as gay as the Christmas lights,
And a picture book of the Arabian nights,
And a painted, silken Chinese fan –
But the one she loved was the nutcracker man.
She thought about him when she went to bed.
With his great long legs and his funny little head.
So she crept downstairs for a last good night,
And arrived in the middle of a furious fight.
The royal mouse that sucked its thumbs
Led an army of mice with swords and drums.

50

They were battling to seize the toys as slaves
To wait upon them in their secret caves.
The nutcracker man cracked many a crown,
But they overwhelmed him, they whelmed him down,
They were cramming him into a hole in the floor
When the little girl tiptoed to the door.
She had one talent which made her proud,
She could miaow like a cat, and now she miaowed.
A miaow so fierce, a maiow so feline,
That the mice fled home in a squealing beeline.
The nutcracker man cracked a hickory nut
To see if his jaws would open and shut,
Then he cracked another and he didn't wince,
And he turned like that! into a handsome prince,
And the toys came dancing from the Christmas tree
To celebrate the famous victory.

OGDEN NASH

It Came Upon the Midnight Clear

It came upon the midnight clear,
That glorious song of old,
From angels bending near the earth
To touch their harps of gold:
'Peace on the earth, good-will to men,
From heav'n's all-gracious King!'
The world in solemn stillness lay
To hear the angels sing.

Still through the cloven skies they come,
With peaceful wings unfurled;
And still their heav'nly music floats
O'er all the weary world;
Above its sad and lowly plains
they bend on hov'ring wing;
And ever o'er its Babel sounds
The blessed angels sing.

Yet with the woes of sin and strife
The world has suffered long;
Beneath the angel-strain have rolled
Two thousand years of wrong;
And man, at war with man, hears not
The love-song which they bring:
O hush the noise ye men of strife,
And hear the angels sing!

For lo! the days are hastening on,
By prophet bards foretold,
When, with the ever-circling years,
Comes round the age of gold;
When peace shall over all the earth
Its ancient splendours fling,
And the whole world send back the song
Which now the angels sing.

E.H. SEERS

52

A COUNTRY CHRISTMAS

(from *A Country Child*)

ALISON UTTLEY

A few days before Christmas Mr Garland and Dan took a bill-hook and knife and went into the woods to cut branches of scarlet-berried holly. They tied them together with ropes and dragged them down over the fields to the barn. Mr Garland cut a bough of mistletoe from the ancient hollow hawthorn which leaned over the wall by the orchard, and thick clumps of dark-berried ivy from the walls.

Indoors, Mrs Garland and Susan and Becky polished and rubbed and cleaned the furniture and brasses, so that everything glowed and glittered. They decorated every room, from the kitchen where every lustre jug had its sprig in its mouth, every brass candlestick had its chaplet, every copper saucepan and preserving pan had its wreath of shining berries and leaves, through the hall, which was a bower of green, to the two parlours which were festooned and hung with holly and boughs of fir, and ivy berries dipped in red raddle, and left over from sheep marking.

On Christmas Eve fires blazed in the kitchen and parlour and even in the bedrooms. Becky ran from room to room with the red-hot salamander which she stuck between the bars to make a blaze, and Mrs Garland took the copper warming pan filled with glowing cinders from the kitchen fire and rubbed it between the sheets of all the beds. Susan had come down to her cosy tiny room with thick curtains at the window, and a fire in the big fireplace. Flames roared up the chimneys as Dan carried in the logs and Becky piled them on the blaze. The wind came back and tried to get in, howling at the key-holes, but all the shutters were cottered and the doors shut. The horses and mares stood in the stables, warm and happy, with nodding heads. The cows slept in the cow-houses, the sheep in the open sheds. Only Rover stood at the door of his kennel, staring up at the sky, howling to the dog in the moon, and then he, too, turned and lay down in his straw.

In the middle of the kitchen ceiling there hung the kissing-branch, the best and brightest pieces of holly made in the shape of a large ball which dangled from the hook. Silver and gilt drops, crimson bells, blue glass trumpets, bright oranges and red polished apples, peeped and glittered through the glossy leaves. Little flags of all nations, but chiefly Turkish for some unknown reason, stuck out like quills on a hedgehog. The lamp hung near, and every little berry, every leaf, every pretty ball and apple had a tiny yellow flame reflected in its heart.

Twisted candles hung down, yellow, red, and blue, unlighted but gay, and on either side was a string of paper lanterns.

So the preparations were made. Susan hung up her stocking at the foot of the bed and fell asleep. But soon singing roused her and she sat, bewildered. Yes, it was the carol-singers.

Outside under the stars she could see the group of men and women, with lanterns throwing beams across the paths and on to the stable door. One man stood apart beating time, another played a fiddle and another had a flute. The rest sang in four parts the Christmas hymns, 'While Shepherds watched', 'O come, all ye faithful', and 'Hark the herald angels sing'.

There was the Star, Susan could see it twinkling and bright in the dark boughs with their white frosted layers; and there was the stable. In a few hours it would be Christmas Day, the best day of all the year.

SLEEP TIGHT, FATHER CHRISTMAS

On Christmas Day while we're all playing:
   Stuffing our faces – in church praying,
You know what Santa Claus is doing?
   (No, not skiing or canoeing);
You may think it's rather boring,
   But he's in bed asleep and snoring!

   Poor old Santa – work's all done.
   Let him sleep while we have fun –
   Deserves it more than anyone.
   Sleep tight, Father Christmas.

COLIN McNAUGHTON

SILENT NIGHT

Silent night, holy night,
   All is calm, all is bright
Round yon virgin mother and child,
   Holy infant so tender and mild,
Sleep in heavenly peace.
Sleep in heavenly peace.

Silent night, holy night,
   Shepherds first saw the sight:
Glories stream from heaven afar,
   Heav'nly hosts sing Alleluia:
Christ the Saviour is born,
Christ the Saviour is born.

Silent night, holy night,
   Son of God, love's pure light,
Radiance beams from thy holy face,
   With the dawn of redeeming grace,
Jesus, Lord, at thy birth,
Jesus, Lord, at thy birth.

JOSEPH MOHR

Index of Authors and First Lines

Acknowledgements

The publisher would like to thank the copyright holders for permission to reproduce the following copyright material:

Rodney Bennett: HarperCollins Publishers Ltd for "A Christmas Tree Song" by Rodney Bennett from *The Book of 1000 Poems*, HarperCollins. **Charles Causley:** David Higham Associates Ltd for "High in the Heaven" from *The Gift of a Lamb* by Charles Causley, Robson Books 1978. Copyright © Charles Causley 1978. **Sue Cowling:** Faber & Faber Ltd for "Country Carol" from *What is a Kumquat?*, Faber & Faber Ltd. Copyright © Sue Cowling. Countee Cullen: Bantam Doubleday Dell Publishing Group Inc. for "Under the Mistletoe" by Countee Cullen. **E.E. Cummings:** W.W. Norton & Company Ltd for "little tree" from *Complete Poems 1904-1962* by E.E. Cummings, edited by George J. Firmage. Copyright © 1925, 1953, 1976, 1991 by the Trustees for the E.E. Cummings Trust and George James Firmage. **Walter de la Mare:** The Literary Trustees of Walter de la Mare, and The Society of Authors as their representative for "Mistletoe" from *The Complete Poems of Walter de la Mare* by Walter de la Mare. Copyright © Walter de la Mare. **Eleanor Farjeon:** David Higham Associates Ltd for "The Children's Carol" from *Eleanor Farjeon's Poems for Children*, and "Christmas Stocking" from Children's Bells: A Selection of Poems by Eleanor Farjeon. Copyright © Eleanor Farjeon. **Aileen Fisher:** The author for "Christmas Secrets" from *Out in the Dark and Daylight* by Aileen Fisher, HarperCollins 1980. Copyright © Aileen Fisher 1980. **Michael Harrison:** The author for "The Christmas Spider" from *Junk Mail* by Michael Harrison, Oxford University Press 1993. Copyright © Michael Harrison 1993. **Margaret Mahy:** J.M. Dent & Sons Ltd for "Christmas in New Zealand" from *The First Margaret Mahy Storybook* by Margaret Mahy, J.M. Dent 1972. Copyright © Margaret Mahy 1972. **David McCord:** Little, Brown & Company for "A Christmas Package" from *Away and Ago: Rhymes of the Never Was and Always Is* by David McCord, Little, Brown. Copyright © David McCord 1979, 1980. **Colin McNaughton:** Walker Books Ltd for "Sleep Tight, Father Christmas" from *Santa Claus is Superman* by Colin McNaughton, Walker Books 1988. Copyright © Colin McNaughton 1988. **Ogden Nash:** Curtis Brown Ltd for "Winter Morning" and "The New Nutcracker Suite" from *Ogden Nash Collected Poems*, J.M. Dent. Copyright © Ogden Nash. **James Reeves:** Laura Cecil Literary Agency and the James Reeves Estate for "Waiting" from *Complete Poems for Children* by James Reeves, Heinemann 1973. Copyright © James Reeves 1973. **Ruth Sawyer:** Laurence Pollinger Ltd for "Christmas Morn" from *The Long Christmas* by Ruth Sawyer, Viking Penguin Inc. 1941. Copyright © Ruth Sawyer 1941. **Dylan Thomas:** David Higham Associates Ltd for "Conversation About Christmas" from *Collected Stories* by Dylan Thomas, J.M. Dent. Copyright © Dylan Thomas. **Alison Uttley:** Faber & Faber Ltd for the extract from *The Country Child* by Alison Uttley, Faber & Faber 1931. Copyright © Alison Uttley 1931. **Valerie Worth:** The Estate of Valerie Worth Bahkle for "Christmas Ornaments" by Valerie Worth. Copyright © Valerie Worth.

Every effort has been made to obtain permission to reproduce copyright material but there may be cases where we have been unable to trace a copyright holder. The publisher will be happy to correct any omissions in future printings.

May you have the gladness of Christmas,
which is hope;
The spirit of Christmas, which is peace;
The heart of Christmas, which is love.